TWO LITTLE GARDENERS

By Margaret Wise Brown and Edith Thacher Hurd
Illustrated by Gertrude Elliott

A GOLDEN BOOK • NEW YORK

Copyright © 1951, renewed 1979 by Random House, Inc. All rights reserved. Published in the United States by Golden Books, an imprint of Random House Children's Books, a division of Random House, Inc., New York. Originally published in 1951 by Simon and Schuster, Inc., and Artists and Writers Guild, Inc. GOLDEN BOOKS, A GOLDEN BOOK, A LITTLE GOLDEN BOOK, the G colophon, and the distinctive gold spine are registered trademarks of Random House, Inc. A Little Golden Book Classic is a trademark of Random House, Inc.
www.goldenbooks.com
www.randomhouse.com/kids
Educators and librarians, for a variety of teaching tools, visit us at www.randomhouse.com/teachers
Library of Congress Control Number: 2004117871
ISBN: 978-0-375-83529-2
Printed in the United States of America
20 19 18 17 16 15

Spring!
The snow melted
A snowdrop came up
A robin hopped
And the worm turned in the ground.

The groundhog cast his shadow, and the two little
gardeners came out of their house to plant their garden.

They turned the earth with a shovel and a fork.
And then they chopped up the earth with a hoe.
And they smoothed out the lumps with a rake.
Until it was soft and smooth with only little lumps in it.
At last it was time to plant round little radish seeds,
Thin black lettuce seeds, round wrinkled pea seeds,

Flat pumpkin seeds, squash seeds, and flat lima bean seeds,
And tiny parsley seeds and tomato plants and potato eyes.

Then the rain came.
And the sun shone.
And the wind came softly blowing through the night.
And the rain and the sun and the soft winds in the night
brought little green sprouts sprouting out through the ground.
Radishes popped up. And parsley curled.

And under the ground the beets turned red,
And the carrots grew yellow,
And the potato sprouts grew bigger.

The worms turned the earth over.
The moles dug about.
And a little mouse built a nest in the grass roots
near a rabbit hole.

And beautiful vegetable flowers came out
Yellow tomato flowers
Big yellow squash flowers
Red bean flowers

White pea flowers and potato flowers
All full of bees,
Their friends the bees.

And the weeds came too.
And they grew and they grew and they grew.
Prickly weeds, tall weeds, feathery weeds.
And they grew and they grew and they grew.
And the two little gardeners said:
"This will never do." And they hoed out the weeds.

Then the sun shone hotter and hotter. No rain.
So they came with their hose and sprinkled the rows
Till the dusty dirt was all dark and damp and wet.

And the vegetables grew and they grew and they grew.
Some grew so high the two little gardeners had to put
up little fences for the peas to grow on, and tall poles
for the beans to climb up, and sticks for the tomatoes
to lean on.
And they made little hills to hold up the corn.

Then came the little birds and fur animals—the gardeners who only come to eat and who come to eat too soon. There were too many creatures in the garden, so the two little gardeners built a big flippy floppy scarecrow.

And a funny fierce-footed "raba-mole" to frighten away certain rabbits and groundhogs and squirrels and moles and field mice who had come to eat up the garden.

Then the garden grew and it grew and it grew.
The corn tassels bloomed,
And the pumpkins got fat.
And the beans grew long
And the carrots pushed up through the ground.
And the cabbages looked like great green roses
all in a row.

Day after day something was ripe and ready to pick.

So the two little gardeners came with their baskets and they picked and they picked and they picked. Pumpkins and parsnips and peppers and cabbages and beans off the poles and potatoes deep down in the ground and the corn from the tall, green corn stalks. Until everything was picked.

And they cooked and they cooked
and they cooked and they cooked,
Pumpkins and potatoes and parsley,
Corn and cabbage and beans,
Until everything was cooked.

And they ate and they ate and they ate and they ate,
Cabbage and carrots and cauliflower
Beets and beans and long ears of corn,
Until they were full.

But they couldn't eat it all.
So they put up some things in cans and jars and bottles
and stored them away on the shelves.

The onions were dried and hung in big bunches.
The carrots were stored in big tubs.
There was a bin for potatoes and a bin for pumpkins
and a high dry shelf for squash.
Then the little gardeners rested.
And they sang a little song.

FULL AS A FIDDLE

Poem by Margaret Wise Brown

Music by Dorothy Cadzow

Hi did-dle did-dle, We're full as a fid-dle Of things that come out of the ground.__ What we plant in the Spring We eat in the Fall And put up in jars And eat it all When the snow comes fall - ing down.

A